4 WICKED WINDS

by

Wayne Kyle Spitzer

Copyright © 2019 Wayne Kyle Spitzer. All Rights Reserved. Published by Hobb's End Books, a division of ACME Sprockets & Visions. Cover design Copyright © 2019 Wayne Kyle Spitzer. Please direct all inquiries to: HobbsEndBooks@yahoo.com

All characters appearing in this work are fictitious. Any resemblance to real persons, living or dead, is purely coincidental. This book contains material protected under International and Federal Copyright Laws and Treaties. Any unauthorized reprint or use of this book is prohibited. No part of this book may be reproduced or transmitted in any form or by any means, electronic or mechanical, including photocopying, recording, or by any information storage and retrieval system without express written permission from the author. This ebook is licensed for your personal enjoyment only. This ebook may not be re-sold or given away to other people. If you would like to share this book with another person, please purchase an additional copy for each recipient. If you are reading this book and did not purchase it, or it was not purchased for your use only, then please purchase your own copy. Thank you for respecting the hard work of this author.

GOLEM

Why did I do it? *Because I was meant to.* Because that's why I had been allowed to live. This was the whole of the affair in one simple statement.

Memory, of course, can be a dodgy thing: why else would my recall of the Benton Boys—and how Old Man Moss had brought their reign of terror to an end—have lain dormant for so long (forty years, to be exact), right up until that moment I saw what I'd at first taken to be a man—but quickly realized was not—ascending the tower crane just beyond our encampment?

The obvious answer is that a lot can happen in forty years. A man could go from being an innocent kid in Benton, Washington (population one-hundred and seventeen) to a scary homeless dude in Seattle—Belltown, to be precise—just as I had. But there's another answer, too, one we don't talk about as much, which is that some things get buried not for any lack of a mental space to put them but for their very unfathomableness and steadfast refusal to make sense. For me, Old Man Moss' handling of the Benton Boys had been just that, something I'd sublimated completely in the years following not because the event—the events—had been forgotten, but because I simply hadn't the means of processing them up until that night; the night I climbed the massive tower crane in downtown Seattle and came face to face with the brute. The night the string of gruesome murders that had plagued the city for months had, at last, come to an end.

"I don't see anything," said Billy the Skid, his boozy breath seeming to billow with each syllable, as he stood beside me and squinted up at the crane. "Who would it be? Construction's been halted for months, even I know that."

"I didn't say 'who,' I said 'what,' as in what is that, right there?" I pointed to where the gray figure could once again be seen (ascending not the ladder inside the scaffolding but the tower itself, like some kind of huge spider). "Do you see it? Like a man, and yet somehow not a man. And look, it's got someone thrown over its shoulder. It's right there, damn you!"

Billy only shook his head. "Whatever you say, boss." He chuckled as he made his way back to his shopping cart. "Someone thrown over his shoulder. I say if you can't handle Thunderbird you ought to leave the drinking to me. Who the hell did 'ya think it was? The Belltown Brute? Ha! And I suppose he …"

But I wasn't listening, not really. I was still watching the gray man, the gray *thing,* ascend the tower—the hammerhead, I've heard them called—its tail swinging like a cobra (yes, yes, it had a *tail*), its ashen skin seeming to catch the lightning and throw it back, its cone-shaped head turning to face me.

Yes. Yes, it could be. Still … was it even possible? Well, no, to be frank—it wasn't. But then, everything about the summer of '79 and what had happened to the Benton Boys and Old Man Moss' ancient Jewish magik had been impossible.

That didn't change the fact that it had happened—and it *had* happened—hadn't it?

I didn't know for sure, no more than I knew whether the entry point to the crane would be locked or if I had the courage to scale the ladder or if lightning would strike as I climbed killing me just as dead as the Benton Boys. In the end I was certain of only one thing—one thing alone as I gazed up at the tower crane and watched its great jib swing in the wind. And that was that if what I suspected was true, I was at least partially responsible—for the Benton Boys, for the string of murders across Seattle and the so-called "Belltown Brute," all of it.

And that meant I had a responsibility to do something. Indeed, that I was the only person who could.

They'd had names, of course. Rusty, Jack, and Colton—otherwise known as the Benton Boys. But their individual identities had long since been subsumed by the group, the pack—I'm sure if you would have caught any single one of them alone they'd have been just as agreeable as could be. The rub, of course, was that they were never alone—that was something those who challenged them learned quickly. I learned it the day I was to meet Colton at the flagpole after school to settle our differences and he didn't show; which left Aaron and I to hoof it home feeling both victorious and relieved, at least, that is, until we rounded his block—and found them waiting for us. All three of them.

I wish I could say I was shocked that Aaron got the worst of it—it was my fight, after all, not his—but the truth of it was the Benton Boys' race-hatred was well known, and they weren't about to miss a chance to thrash a genuine Jew. Not when his idiot friend had created such a perfect opportunity. And so the racial epitaphs flew, faster even than the Boys' fists—kike, shylock, yid, Christ-killer, a few I'd never even heard before—and poor Aaron bled, and by the time it was done we'd both suffered concussions and Aaron had lost a tooth and Old Man Moss had begun screaming—in Yiddish—from his door, calling the Boys chazers and hitsigers and paskudniks, and informing them the police were already on their way. Which they weren't, actually, because Old Man Moss didn't trust anyone in a uniform.

Regardless, the Benton Boys promptly fled, and after a brief sojourn in the emergency room we were back in Aaron's front yard—just sitting there on the porch with his parents and watching the shadows lengthen across the grass. That's when I first heard his old man utter the word "golem," which he pronounced *goy-lem,* drawing a stern rebuke from Aaron's mother, who said, quickly, "Feh! And bring tsores upon us? Oy vey! *Mishegas."*

The Old Man only snorted. "It is Mishegas to do nothing." He stroked Aaron's hair absently.

"No. An eye for an eye. A tooth for an actual tooth."

"Bubbala ..."

"No. *Meesa masheena.* So it will be."

And nothing more was said—not by the Old Man or by Aaron's mother or by anyone present at all.

By the time I saw Old Man Moss again, Spring was moving rapidly toward Summer and we'd been out of school for nearly two weeks—long enough to have already tired of jumping into the river and/or bicycling out to Shelly Lake; which, in case you were wondering, were the only things to do in Benton, during that summer or any other. I was luckier than most in that I had a lawn mowing business to occupy my time—mostly for friends and family, the Mosses included—which is what I was doing when Aaron tapped me on the shoulder and asked if I could lend he and his father a quick hand.

"Is it out of this heat?" I remember shouting over the lawnmower—which was louder than most—the sweat running in rivers down my face and arms, "Because I'm dying here, and that's no joke."

"It's right here, in the garage," he said breezily, but seemed uneasy as I killed the motor and sponged my brow. "Look ... not a word about this, okay? And, please, don't laugh. Whatever you do. He—he's touchy about his art."

I think I just looked at him. It was fine by me; I'd no idea he was even an artist. "Sure, man. No problem." I must have leaned toward him. "What is it? Some kind of naked pictures?"

He blushed and stepped back. "No, man. Jesus. But it is—strange. Not a word now, okay?"

"Not a word," I promised, and gave him a salute.

It's funny—because the first thing I noticed upon stepping into the garage wasn't the fact that Old Man Moss was holding what appeared to be massive gray arm in his hands. Nor was it the fact that in the middle of the room stood an 8-foot-tall giant—a giant which appeared to have been fashioned from solid clay and resembled not so much a man but a hulking, naked ape. Nor was it even the thing's frightful visage or stoic, lifeless, outsized eyes.

No, it was the fact that the room was illuminated by candles and candelabrums—as opposed to bulbs or work lights or sun seeping through windows (all of which had been covered with what appeared to be black sheets). It was the fact that the garage didn't look like a garage. It looked—for all intents and purposes—like a temple.

"Ah, Thomas, by boy! *Vus machs da!* You are just in time."

It was on the tips of my lips to ask him what for when he handed me the arm, which was surprisingly heavy. "I'll need you and Aaron to hold this while I sculpt. Can you do that?"

The clay was tacky and moist beneath my fingers. I looked at Aaron, who looked back at me as if to say, *Just go with it. Humor him.*

"Sure, Mr. Moss. But—" I followed Aaron's lead as he positioned the arm against the mock brute's shoulder. "What on earth *is* it?"

His face beamed with pride as he worked the leaden clay. "Why, this is Yossele—but you may call him Josef. And he is what the rabbis of Chelm and Prague called a golem—a being created from inanimate matter. This one is devoted to *tzedakah,* or justice."

At last he stepped back and appeared to scrutinize his work. "And justice is precisely what he will bring—once he is finished. Once the *shem* has been placed in his mouth." He took a deep breath and exhaled, tentatively. "Okay, boys … you can let go. Slowly."

I didn't know what justice had to do with art, but we did so—the clammy clay wanting to stick to our fingers, its moist touch seeming hesitant to break contact. "Aaron, won't you be a good *boychick* and bring me the *shem*. Easy does it, now. Don't drop it."

I watched as Aaron approached one of the workbenches and fetched an intricately-crafted gold box.

"Ah, yes. The *shem,* you see, is what gives the golem its power—thank you, son, *a sheynem dank*. It is what gives it the ability to move and become animated."

I glanced at Aaron, who only looked back at me uncertainly, as his father approached the golem and opened the box, the gold plating of which gleamed like a fire before the candelabrums. "This one consists of only one word—one of the Names of God, which is too sacred to be uttered here." He withdrew a slip of paper and placed it into the golem's mouth. "I shall only say *emet,* which means 'truth' … and have done with it. And so it is finished. *Tetelestai."* He turned and looked directly at me, I have no idea why. "The debt will be paid in full."

Nobody said anything for a long time, even as the birds tweeted outside and a siren wailed somewhere in the distance. We just stood there and stared at his creation.

At last I said, "So are you going to enter in the Fair, Mr. Moss, or what? How will you even move it?"

At which Old Man Moss only smiled, ruffling my hair, and said, "No—it is only for this moment. That is the nature of Art. *Tsaytvaylik.* Tomorrow it will be gone. Now run along and finish your lawn. I've involved you enough."

And the next day it *was* gone, at least according to Aaron, and both of us, I think, promptly forgot about it. At least until the first of the Benton Boys turned up dead, Sheriff Donner directing the recovery while his ashen-blue body bobbed listlessly against the Benedict A. Saltweather Dam.

It was June.

By July, the body of a second Benton Boy had been discovered—my very own buddy, Colton.

They'd found him in a stone quarry about fifteen miles from town—the Eureka Tile Company, as I recall—his limbs broken and bent back on themselves ("like some discarded Raggedy Ann," wrote the local paper) and his head completely gone—which caused a real sensation amongst the townsfolk as each attempted to solve the riddle and at least one woman reported having seen it: "Just floating down the river, like a pale, blue ball."

But it wasn't until Rusty was killed that things reached a fever pitch, with Sheriff Donner under attack for failing to solve the case and neighbor turning against neighbor in a kind of collective paranoia—for by this point no one could be trusted, not in such a small town, and the killer or killers might be anyone, even your spouse or best friend.

It was against this backdrop that I was able to break from my lawn duties—which had exploded like gangbusters over the summer—long enough to visit the Mosses: which would have been the day before Independence Day, 1979. A Tuesday, as I recall. It's funny I should remember that. Aaron's mother was working in her vegetable garden—just bent over her radishes like an emaciated old crone—when I arrived, and didn't even look up when I asked if Aaron was around. "He's in his room—done sick with the flu. Best put on a mask before you go." She added: "You'll find some in the kitchen."

I think I just looked at her—at her curved spine and thin ankles, her tied up hair which had gone gray as a golem. Then I went into the house and made my way toward Aaron's room, passing his parents' quarters—upon which had been hung a 'Do Not Disturb' sign and a Star of David—on the way. I didn't bother fetching a mask; I'm not sure why—maybe it was because I was already convinced that whatever Aaron had, I had too. Maybe it was because I was already convinced that by participating in the ritual we'd somehow brought a curse upon us—a curse upon Benton—that it had never been just 'art' and that it could never be atoned for, not by Aaron or myself or Old Man Moss or anybody. That we'd blasphemed the Name of the Lord and would now have to pay, just as Jack had paid, just as Colton had paid. Just as Rusty had paid when they'd found him with his intestines wrapped around his throat and his eyeballs gouged out.

"Shut the door, please. Quickly," said Aaron as I stepped into his room—immediately noticing how dark it was, and that the windows had been completely blacked out (with the same sheets from the garage, I presumed). He added: "The light ... It—it's like it eats my eyes."

Christ—I *know*. But that's what he said: *Like it ate his eyes.*

I stumbled into a stool in the dark—it was right next to his bed—and sat down. Nor were the black sheets thick enough to completely choke the light, so that as I looked at him he began to manifest into something with an approximate shape: something I dare say was not entirely human—a thing thick and rounded and gray as the dead, like a huge misshapen rock, perhaps, or a mass of potter's clay, but with eyes. Then again it was dark enough so that I may only have imagined it—who's to say after forty years?

"Jesus, dude. What's happened to you? And where's your dad? I saw a 'Do Not Disturb' sign on his door. Is he—"

"Like me, only worse," choked Aaron, and then coughed—wetly, stickily. "Listen. I haven't much time. Do you remember the ritual … and how we inserted the *shem* into the golem's mouth?"

"Of course," I said—and immediately started shaking my head. "Now wait a minute. You don't really think—"

"Shut up, man. Just *shut the fuck up.* This is important. The Benton Boys—what's happened to us—it's not a coincidence, okay? Dad—he created a golem … do you understand? Not a work of art—not what Ms. Dickerson calls a metaphor. But a genuine, animate golem—right out of the folklore. Now, my mother called Rabbi Weiss when the murders started happening and told him what she suspected—that my dad had created Josef to avenge the Benton Boys' attack on us. And do you know what he said?"

"Aaron, Jesus, man—"

"He said this type of golem would go on killing, that it wouldn't stop with just the Benton Boys but would continue on to different towns and cities—for months, years, even decades. That it could make itself invisible—at least to anyone who hadn't a hand in creating it—and thus go about killing with complete efficiency; and that not even bullets could stop it, only the hand of its creator or someone who had assisted in that creation—by removing from its mouth the one thing that allowed it to move in the first place ... the Holy Shem, the slip of parchment upon which was written one of the secret Names of God."

He gripped my arm suddenly and I could tell by his cold, clammy embrace that it wouldn't be long; that his flesh had become like clay and his blood had turned thick as mud. "It's you, Thomas, don't you see? You! Only you can stop it now, only you can—"

But I didn't hear anything else he had to say, for I'd scrambled to the door and burst back into the hall. And then I ran, ran as though the world could not contain me, faster and faster and further yet—across forty years and from every type of responsibility—into drugs and alcohol and the cold numbness of the streets. Into a dream of forgetfulness which ended only when I saw the man who was not a man scaling the ghostly tower crane near our ramshackle encampment in Belltown. Until I went to the base of it, and, finding its gate lazed open, mounted the ladder at its center. And began to climb.

I was nearing the top—although still a good fifty feet away—when there was a sound, a series of sounds, actually, *thunk—thunk—thunk,* like a ham bouncing down metal stairs, and something sprinkled my face. That's when I realized that what had fallen (and bounced off the beams) was in fact a human head. By then, of course, it was gone, and I was continuing my ascent: trying not to acknowledge how the city had become so small or that lightning could strike at any instant or that the shaft of the crane was swaying woozily in the wind. Trying and mostly succeeding—at least, that is, until I reached the top, whence I climbed onto the platform next to the operator's cab (which was hanging wide open) and proceeded to vomit, although whether it was from a fear of heights or the smell of decomposition from the cab I couldn't have said.

Nor was I surprised to find that the compartment was stuffed full of bodies and body parts, like a veritable meat locker ... filled with arms and legs and heads and torsos ... or that when I turned away to retch again I saw the golem itself at the end of the crane's long jib—just crouched there in a kind of lotus position, as if he—it—were meditating. As if it—he—were waiting for me.

I can see you, Josef, I thought as the American flag crackled at the back of the crane and the great jib swung languidly in the wind ... *Can you see me?*

And then I began moving forward, slowly, tentatively—the rails of the jib like ice beneath my grip.

You can, can't you? I thought, and knew that it was so. *Tell me, Josef. Why is it you think I was spared—why I've been spared all these years—when your other creators were turned into little more than pillars of salt? Have you ever thought about that?*

Lightning flashed in the distance and turned everything white—turned the golem white—so that its monstrous features fell into stark relief; so that its cone-shaped head shown like a knife.

We are bound together, after all—don't pretend I don't know that. Even as I know you can hear me—just as plain as though I were speaking. And I ask you again—have you thought about it? Because I have.

Thunder rumbled as I drew to within twenty feet of him and paused, wondering just how I would go about it, how I would remove the *shem*. At last I said, "You were created not by God but by a man and the sages before him—now you must return to your dust. Do you understand that? It is not now, nor has it ever been—nor will it ever be—your earth to walk. It is time to go, Josef. It is long past time."

He—it—whatever—just looked at me, its slanted gray eyes inert, uninhabited—lifeless—and yet, *not*. And it occurred to me that creation was itself a kind of blasphemy; a fracturing of some perfect, unfathomable thing into something separate and purely reducible—something alone, something apart. That it was, in a sense, a cruelty. And if that were the case—wasn't it at least possible that the golem—

But then it was *moving*—suddenly, impossibly, and I was stumbling back along the gangway, and before I could do much of anything it had leapt upon me and begun gnashing its teeth—at which instant I jammed my fist into its mouth and groped for the *shem,* and whereupon finding it, yanked it free.

At that it had simply collapsed, its full weight pinning me to the gangway, and its body had broken apart like so much old masonry as its arms and legs snapped in two and its head rolled back from its shoulders—to promptly shatter against the steel mesh floor.

That's when the rains came, washing away the clay and drenching my hair and clothes, which were a beggar's clothes, until finally I rolled upon the gangway and peered down at our encampment—which was visible only because of Billy the Skid's battery-powered light—and realized, abruptly, that I still gripped the *shem*. The Holy Shem.

The Secret Name of God.

I didn't move, didn't breath, for what seemed a long time. In the end, I merely turned my fist and opened it—letting the slip of parchment fall. Watching as it fluttered into the void.

And then I slept.

At length I dreamed, of Benton and summer and freshly-cut grass ... and the first time I'd had matzo; as well as of Aaron and his parents and my parents too, whom I hadn't seen or dreamed of in years.

And when at last I awakened I did so not to the gray ceiling of my tent but a swirl of seagulls and the entire sky.

ALUKA

Malachi suspects something—has suspected, it's clear to me now, since the raid on Medea Coven. I can see it in his eyes as we stare at each other across the War Wagon: something cool, dispassionate (even behind the smoked lenses of his gas mask), predatory, like a cat. He is on to something, he knows.

My headset crackles as the driver updates our status: "Fifteen minutes to target. Check your belts and harnesses—it's going to get bumpy."

I check my belt and harness, the wagon starting to rock, our tanks clinking and sloshing. Jeremiah offers me a stick of gum—but I shake my head. Nobody says anything.

"Remember, we're going in fast and we're going in hot," crackles Patrobus (as though he has taken up residence in our very minds), "Look sharp. And don't get so preoccupied with your kill count that you forget; this is an *intelligence* op. Find the lab, extract what you can, air it out, and then *get out*. Is that clear?"

Although he doesn't mention him by name we all know who he's referring to: Malachi, who once let a witch escape just so he could prolong the pursuit. A *witch*. A woman. A carrier of the M24 virus. Something to be killed on sight.

"It is clear, Captain," says Jeremiah, glancing at his friend—at Malachi. "I'll make sure Doctor Aluka leaves him some targets. We'll keep him occupied."

"Find the lab, Jeremiah. Find out what it is they've been doing there. Then get your men back on this side of the Transom."

And then he is gone and there is just the twelve of us, our buckled hats canted low on our brows, our flame-retardant Puritan tunics black as night and white as snow, our muskets charged and ready to spew fire.

At which moment Malachi just looks at me, seeming to smirk behind his mask (which has been spit shined to a gloss), and says, "How about it,

Brother Aluka? A contest! Who can kill the most women? That is—if you still have the jewels for it."

"Lay off him," says Jeremiah. "The Medea raid was tough on everyone. Besides, his record's better than any of us."

But I don't say anything, only use the time remaining to dissemble and clean my weapon, wondering: What did he see and how much does he know? And what will happen when I can no longer hide my eyes—which have begun to turn white when I sleep, witch's white, and take longer to clear each morning? How long is it until I—who am not fully man nor fully woman—have at last become neither; neither male nor female, neither Witch Doctor or witch?

They don't know, of course. That I am so-called intersex. How could they? When I first came to the guild I had yet to even reach puberty, therefore my feminine attributes had yet to develop and I was diagnosed instead with a mild form of AIS, or androgen insensitivity syndrome. My face, in short, resembled a woman—at least, more so than it did a man's. Nor was I drafted at the age of twelve as are most Witch Doctors—or so I've been told—but rather just showed up one day at the station-house: starving, dehydrated, dressed in rags. Lost. If not for Doctor Patrobus—who was not yet even a captain but argued effectively for my indoctrination—I would have perished. As for my life before that time, I have little memory. Only vignettes, which come to me in the twilight between sleep and wakefulness and—bearing more in common with dreams than truth—are best forgotten.

Concealing my identity from my fellow doctors, meanwhile, has not been difficult, for it is the expectation amongst the men of New Salem that everyone should become self-sufficient—and at the youngest age possible—thus, I have lived alone in a cottage near the station-house for nearly twenty years—and have never had to shower or otherwise disrobe in their presence. Only the machine men and women of the brothel know for certain (one man and two women, to be precise), and they do not speak, save for the words for which they've been programmed. And so my secrets have been kept safe even while my identity has been tested—enough so that I had determined myself to be a heterosexual male in a half-female body; feminine, it is true, and yet, psychologically, all male. All witch doctor.

Until, that was, the raid on Medea Coven. Until the oddly boyish girl in the crystalline shower—that haunted, singular girl, who's eyes might have been a lover's and yet, queerly, a sister's too. The pale girl with the pale, milky, alabaster eyes—though not quite white. The witch with the labrys tattoo.

They swarm me like wasps the instant the elevator doors open, pale hands groping, white eyes flashing—and the raid on Medea, which has already been a disaster, becomes very nearly a route. In the end all I can do is to open my musket—even as they claw and tear at my clothing—and bathe the compartment in flame; hoping the fireproof quilting of my vest will protect me now that it has been so gravely compromised.

Somehow, it works—and I am able to climb out from beneath them, triggering the doors behind me before any can escape to continue their attack. (As Captain Patrobus likes to say: "A burning witch is not a dead witch—it is, however, a pissed off one.")

Then the car is descending and I am clasping my tunic—which has been ripped open to expose a breast—knowing that if I am to sweep and clear the floor I will have to do so one-handed—something I am not sure I can do. But the Captain—my Captain!—is counting on me; this much I know too, as are Jeremiah and the others (whether they would admit to it or not). And so I push on to the first unit (the coven has squatted in an abandoned luxury hotel) and kick in its door—where, having begun to squeeze the trigger, I first glimpse the girl in the crystalline shower (by which I mean a shower so exquisite it seems to have been hewn from some great diamond rather than constructed of metal and glass; a shower, oddly, which stands at the very center of the room); and where, inexplicably, I pause. For she is looking directly at me.

It is a mystery—why I do not fire. Why I do not simply squeeze the trigger and send an explosive projectile hurtling into the glass. Why I don't just drench the room in fire and smoke and quickly move onto the next: sweeping each and every unit, clearing the entire floor. Instead I find myself barking at her, ordering her, shouting for her to *get out, get down, down upon the floor—hurry, hurry, do it now!*

But she does not listen, only gently turns the taps, then, reaching for her towel, wraps it about herself and exits the stall—calmly, serenely—until she is standing before me and simply staring, her eyes beginning to widen, her expression one of complete puzzlement. And it is at this moment and none before that I realize that, in my haste and terror, I have gripped my weapon in both hands—allowing the torn flap of uniform to fall. Allowing my breast to fall and be visible. And though I push it back up immediately and press it to my chest, the damage has been done; so much so that the girl feels emboldened to approach me, to enter my immediate space, to reach up and to touch my mask, feeling its rubbery flesh, tracing its cruel contours, as though I were a book of Braille beneath her fingers.

"You poor, poor, pitiable thing. How lost you must feel. How lonely. What have they done to you, that you could do this? That you could eat your own so—willingly. How did they break you so completely?"

But I am frozen, paralyzed, managing only to divert me eyes, managing only to note the tattoo on her shoulder: two female symbols entwined, what is known as a labrys—the symbol of female solidarity, the symbol of mutual Eros. And I feel myself coming undone, feel my hand lower and the torn fabric fall, feel my legs buckle like so much rubber until I collapse against the floor in a jangling heap and she reaches out to me in a way no one has ever reached out to me, feeling my pain, anticipating its reach, empathizing as though I were a sister, touching me as though my weakness could not only be forgiven but was to be expected, as though—

And her head simply explodes—blasting apart like a watermelon, speckling the lenses of my gasmask with blood, spattering the crystalline shower like shot. And when I look behind me I see Malachi seeming to laugh through his mask;

laughing and feigning to blow on his gun, before twirling it like a gunslinger and depositing it into its holster.

After which he says, "And an Empath makes twenty. Oh, Aluka! If I didn't know better I'd say you were about to dance!"

He goes to the girl's flaming corpse, and, snatching up her towel—which has somehow survived the blast—begins beating out the flames. What he does not do is to help me up. What he does not do is ask me if I'm all right.

I clasp my uniform against my chest and stand, hoping he hasn't seen anything, hoping he is just as self-absorbed as he seems, praying he has paid no witness to my failure. At last he asks, "Do we need a medic, is that it? You look as though you've been shot. Let me have a look—"

I jerk away before he is able to touch me, gripping my uniform like a vise, retreating back through the door.

"It's nothing," I say, "Screamers outside the elevator. It's just—just a flesh wound. Where's Jeremiah?"

He pauses, abruptly, as though it wouldn't have occurred to him to ask that, not in a thousand years. "He's—being Jeremiah, killing witches on the seventh floor. What am I, his mother?" He looks me up and down once—twice. "Are you good to go, or what? We've still got the rest of this floor to clear."

I hold my uniform, feeling suddenly nauseous, suddenly disoriented. "Maybe—maybe it's worse than I thought. Maybe—can you handle it, you think?"

That's when I see it—the first sign of real unease, the first inkling that there is something amiss, something not right—something he should be seeing, but cannot. Then he is gone—out the doorway and down the hall, after which I hear a door being kicked in and a series of blasts, which echo throughout the corridor like thunder. Which reverberate from the walls like a storm.

We are close enough now that the driver has activated the loudspeakers: *Ohhh, myyy love, my darling, I've hungered for your touch ...*

It is time; there's a riot of clicks and ca-chinks as everyone primes their muskets, pressurizes their masks. I double check my grip reservoir (crucial in the event one gets separated from their tank): it is full.

And time ... goes by ... so slowly ...

I notice a few disconnect their arm hoses—Malachi, Ishmael, Artemas—against regulation but a favorite hack, for it allows the musket to be switched from hand to hand or spun like a wheel from its ring lever. The problem is that witches have been known to use telekinesis to snatch the weapons away—that and the fact that the grip has limited capacity and reseating it can take precious seconds.

And then we are there, we are at the former hospital—the wagon lurching to a stop, the rear doors banging open—and everyone is unbuckling, piling out.

"Let's go, let's go, let's go!" shouts Jeremiah, even as the first charges are thrown and detonate against the doors—blasting them to smithereens, rocking the grounds like an earthquake. "Aluka, Malachi, Lazarus—levels 3 through 4, go! Ishmael, Silas, Artemas, come with me."

Ohhh, myyy love, my darling ...

We enter the foyer—fanning out like black specters, winding up staircases, pouring into hallways, as the first of the witches are lit up like little suns and a collective gasp echoes throughout the building. Seconds later the screaming begins, the shrieks, the mournful wailing, like mothers over dead children.

I focus on locating the lab—knowing Malachi will clear the floor; knowing he will leave nothing standing.

The truth is I don't know if I can still do it: kill witches, murder women. The truth is something has awakened that I cannot put back to sleep—something ghostly, elusive, something I cannot parse or ration away.

I push it from my mind, ducking into a side corridor, an inner voice seeming to tell me what to do, where to go, as if a kind of third ear has opened, *a third eye*—a window into the world of the witches.

The blue door at the end of the hall, the voice seems to say, the *voices,* rather. *Do you remember? We put it in ourselves—the witches of Scarth Coven—put it in to withstand the blast of their muskets. But you know the code; it is embedded in the hive. Just use your intuition, and let thy hand by thy guide.*

And then I am there and am punching in the code—66-67-66—understanding not at all what has happened; as the lock mechanism buzzes and the bolt retracts. As the door swings open and the lab, so long and white and evenly-lit (precisely as it appeared in the spy photos), so incongruous with everything we thought we knew about the witches, appears.

Nor is it unoccupied—for a woman has approached in the time it's taken me to stand there; a tall woman with long, straight, black hair and eyes as white as her smock—a High Witch as far removed from the screamers as is a human from a chimpanzee. I train my weapon on her.

"Based on the fact that you have not yet incinerated everything," she says, her voice calm, clear, mellifluous, "I'll take it you are surprised." Then she laughs a little. "What did you expect, a boiling cauldron?"

I look at her, saying nothing.

She adds, "I must say, *I* am surprised. By you. Some things never change. We still underestimate each other. Women and men."

She moves the hair away from her eyes and regards me—coolly, clinically. "How did you know? The code, our very existence … It seems, improbable."

I glance about the room: at the vertical glass tanks containing dyed water and floating cadavers (both male and female). At the jars containing fetuses and inner reproductive organs and phalluses.

"Information," I say. "Program objectives. Military applications. Outcomes. For your life."

She doesn't move, doesn't blink. "We both know that isn't going to happen … *Witch Doctor.*"

I stare at her as muskets discharge in the distance and grenade blasts rock the building. At last I reach up with my free hand and decompress the mask … then take it off completely and swing it around to my back. "Perhaps I'm not asking as a Witch Doctor. Or even a man."

She looks at me incredulously, disbelievingly, then, suddenly, rushes to within several feet of me, where she pauses. "You're ... But—your voice, *your eyes.* How could a woman have clear—"

I only shake my head.

Slowly, it dawns on her, spilling across her face like the sun, illuminating her eyes. "Oh, my God." She sways as though she might fall upon the floor; then, recovering, begins pacing back and forth. "I mean, what are the odds ..."

"You begin to see my interest," I say, even as my finger tightens against the trigger. "Now—again. Your life for information. What is all this about?"

She stops pacing suddenly, her face a riot of emotions, as though she is experiencing some kind of epiphany. "But, don't you see?" She gestures at the tanks and jars. *"You're* what all this is about. Facial reconstruction, breast reduction, eye normalization—all attempts to place spies amongst your ranks; to infiltrate you, as you have infiltrated us."

She steps to within a few feet of me. "The Power—do you have it? How about identity? Orientation? Do they know—the men, that is—do they accept it?"

I hesitate, questioning my own motives. At last I say, "No, they do not—know, that is. I came to them before puberty. As for acceptance, they accept that I am a man with androgen insensitivity syndrome; a man who's face resembles a woman's. That is all. As for having the Power ... my eyes have begun to change, at night, but clearing as the day goes on—if that's what you mean. Now ... please. Details."

She looks at me as though having achieved a minor victory. "That's how you found me, by accessing the hive mind, though you wouldn't have been aware of it. So, you've stayed among them and killed for them in order to survive, but now all that's changing. Isn't it?"

I don't say anything, only continue to stare at her.

"And it *is* changing—make no mistake. That's how M24 progresses. Your eyes will remain white longer with each passing day—until the transformation is at last complete." She scans my face as though attempting to read my thoughts. "Tell me, Witch Doctor. What will you do when that day arrives?"

I say nothing, even as my skin begins to twitch, my musket begins to waver.

"What kind of mercy do you expect from men who have sworn to kill witches on sight, even were it their own mother? Do you presume to think that they shall make an exception for you, and you alone? Or have you considered another way, the only way ... the way of the witches, the way of women. Have you considered following your will to survive unto us—we who will accept you without question and offer you a safe haven amidst the conflict?"

I listen, no longer certain if I am just playing along or not. At last I say, "In return for information, of course."

"Of course," she says, "we are at war. And not just information—but service. For a time, at least."

"You want me to spy, then." I shake my head. "Refuse. For one, the whitening of my eyes is occurring too rapidly. For two, I could never—"

"We have developed a serum for that," she says, and points to a row of vials along the wall. "M-6. It is crude—untested—but it is my belief that it will work."

To my own amazement, I begin lowering my weapon, slowly, tentatively. "And after this period of service … you would welcome me into your fold. Knowing I am neither male nor female. Knowing I am neither witch nor—"

"But you *are* a witch, Aluka," she says—and, noticing my reaction, adds: "I have reached into your mind for your name, I am sorry. It was not hard to do—you are one of us now. And we accept all who have been blessed by M24; every living thing—we would accept a man, if he was so gifted."

She extends her hand—languidly, gracefully—smiling beatifically, her hair and skin seeming to shine. "Give me your weapon, Aluka. It is no longer needed. Come home, come home—to how it was in the womb. How it was intended …"

She touches my testicles through my clothing, seeming almost to fondle them, almost to be initiating intimacy, as I drop my weapon to the floor and look into her eyes—finding them beautiful beyond measure, wise beyond comprehension. Hypnotizing …

"As the Goddess says," she whispers, her hand raising to my manhood, touching its shaft, 'If thine eye offends thee—pluck it out. So, too, if thine sword, thine weapon, causes ye to do harm," She grips me suddenly and violently. "Ye must cut it from thine body—yea, cast it before the swine!"

And then I am being electrified from groin to crown, her façade of beauty falling away, her eyes seeming to glow like hot coals, her mouth lazing open as the burning, black bile erupts toward my face—and I duck, rolling, snatching up my weapon, firing from the floor, lighting her up like a Christmas tree.

I waste no time but instead scramble to my feet, rushing toward the vials she indicated, even as she spins about the room, screaming and flailing, knocking over Bunsen burners, smashing test tubes. I spot it instantly—M-6, the serum which can conceal the eyes—and snatch it up, stuffing it into my tunic, ensuring it cannot be seen. Then I back toward the door, opening my musket wide, drenching the lab in flame, causing the tanks holding the cadavers to boil and explode and spill their specimens, setting off a series of blasts as chemicals throughout the lab are super-heated and ignited. And I have but turned to go when I am suddenly faced with a wall of witches—screamers, naturally—crowding in from the hall, groping at my accouterments, tearing open the vest where I'd repaired it, toppling me backward so that I crash upon my tank.

I swipe the musket left to right, igniting them one by one, bursting their eyes, causing them to squeal like pigs. Then I am up and scrambling, through the door and into the hall, where I am once again blocked—for his confrontational posture is clear—this time by Malachi, who has taken off his mask and is smiling at me—smirking—chewing gum. Training his weapon.

"Not so fast, Aluka," he says, chomping on the gum, his eyes sparkling. "I think, just now, that you should drop your weapon. Can you do that for me? Be a sport now—this is awkward enough. Let us make no more messes. Not today. Just drop it, and we shall go."

I look at him for what seems a long time, weighing my options, formulating responses, until, feeling as though something is different, I reach up—and touch my exposed breast.

Malachi only nods, seeming almost regretful, almost empathetic.

I drop my weapon.

"How long have you known?" I ask, wondering how Patrobus will respond, and will I at least be given a dignified death?

"I've suspected from the beginning, if you need to know," he says, adding: "The Medea raid only confirmed it." He studies me as though I were a marvel, shaking his head. "Patrobus' favorite pupil. His pet! Not a man with AIS but a woman, in truth—deceitful by nature, treacherous by impulse—and pre-M24, no doubt. Think of it: M24, in the very heart of New Salem!"

"No, it's not that simple. I—"

"Patrobus will decide, once he knows the truth. Now. Come with me."

"Malachi! Aluka! Is that you down there?"

Jeremiah, at the end of the smoke-filled hall—coming to investigate. Coming toward us.

What happens next happens very quickly, so quickly I cannot recall having actually decided to do it—instead it just flows over and through me until I am reaching toward Malachi and his gun is flying from his hand, flashing through the air like a missile, slapping into my own, at which instant I squeeze the trigger and his head simply explodes, his body bursting into flame, the tank on his back combusting.

Then it is over and I have adjusted the musket for maximum heat, whipping it back and forth over his crumpled body, incinerating him completely, as Jeremiah jogs up and asks me if I am okay, if I have seen Malachi, if the burning room behind me was in fact the lab ... until, noticing my torn uniform and exposed breast, he falls silent. Silent as the grave as I clasp the rent fabric and nudge it back into place. As I look at him and see myself reflected in the lenses of his gas mask—the large brown eyes, not yet white, the tangle of reddish-brown hair.

"We took the lab together," I lie, "but, I'm sorry, Jeremiah."

He looks beyond me, at the burning lab, the clouds of chemical gas, then at the ashes strewn all about the floor. At last he puts a hand over the side of his mask, as though receiving a transmission. "Yes, yes. Yes, it's been completely aired out. Yes, unfortunately. KIA include doctors Silas and Malachi."

I wait, knowing my fate is in his hands. Knowing I could never kill him—not Jeremiah—to save myself. That I am a liar, it is true, and a freak, but a *human,* nonetheless. A man. A woman. But not, as yet, a witch. Not, as yet, a monster.

"Doctors Malachi and Aluka, who is right here beside me," answers Jeremiah. He looks at me blankly, stoically, his expression impossible to read. "Yes, sir. I will. Jeremiah out."

And we just look at each other, the building eerily silent, the raid over, the killing done. At last he says, "You've been promoted to alternate Lead, directly after me." And extends his gloved hand—which I take.

And then we are heading back, back to the War Wagon, across the Transom and the shattered wastes, back to the clean, sterile station house and New Salem.

CRASH DIVE

T-minus 15 and counting. All set there, Chief?

I look at my reflection in the cockpit's front window—the tired eyes, the premature wrinkles and crow's feet—and beyond: to the blue hole and return mirror—which will remain invisible to the naked eye until I am almost upon it.

Roger that. All systems are go and I am hot to drop.

Roger that, *Diver 7*. Nine and counting: 8 … 7 … 6 …

I brace myself as the launch indicator switches from red to green—like a streetlight in the void—and the helmet's blue visor lowers … locking into place.

2 … 1 …

I grip the Jesus handles.

Launch.

Elton John once sang, "And all this science, I don't understand. It's just my job five days a week." That's how it is when you're a Crash Diver: you don't need to understand blue holes or how they differ from wormholes and black holes or what a mobius mirror does—only that it *must* work, every time—because, at the end of the day, that isn't your job. Your job is to be a guinea pig: to be shot into the vortex at near light speed and experience what effect blue hole-assisted mirror travel has on the human body and psyche. Your job is to penetrate to whatever depth they've set the mirror—and, if you're lucky, to enter that mirror and get bounced back.

It hasn't always been like this. Before there was *Zebra Station*—with its luxurious gravity centrifuge and its row of black and yellow delta divers hanging like bats from the launch jib—there was *Blue One,* a sparsely-manned outpost which had sent the first human souls into the maw of the blue hole, men who had come back white-haired and emaciated, debilitated—mentally and physically—mad.

The Crash Diver Program changed all that. From now on only specially-trained pilots would be sent into the Hole, pilots who had the benefit of the first men's experiences as well as spacecraft designed specifically for the task. A lot was learned in a very short time—one of these things was that men who entered the vortex experienced a series of hallucinations, or Dive Visions, in which they briefly felt they had become someone or something else: a soldier in the Holy Roman Army, say, or a person of the opposite sex. Some even purported to have become animals or alien lifeforms—it was the latter which had apparently driven the men of *Blue One* clinically insane.

Another lesson was the fact that the farther a mirror was projected into the vortex the farther it could "cast" to its attendant portal; meaning the Hole might well hold the key to intergalactic space travel. This more than anything had accounted for the program's generous funding, not to mention its exhaustive launch table, which sometimes saw us drop as many as three times in a week. The chief problem, however, remained—and that was that the deeper one dropped, the more acute the hallucinations; hence, the missions had become increasingly volatile, increasingly dangerous.

Regardless, a decision had been made to make the next drop the deepest yet: all the way through the ergosphere—right up to the outer event horizon. By which they meant right up to the point of no return, even by mirror refraction.

And I was the one who drew the unlucky straw.

It is raining. That's the first thing I notice, the first thing that tells me I am no longer in the cockpit. The second is that I'm bleeding—bleeding from the leg, which is making it difficult to press the attack. The third is that I'm dying—as is my opponent—dying beneath a blood red sky.

"It is finished," he says, stumbling forward and back—his blood flowing freely, his hair matted in sweat. "Look at you! Your broadsword is shattered. Your armor is compromised. Why is it you continue?"

But I do not know why I continue—only that I was a Crash Diver once and will be so again, and so must face the vision, endure its consequences. Endure them so that future generations may bridge the gulf of galaxies!

At last I say: "Are you better off? We die together, Sir Aglovere. Surely you—"

But I am baffled by my own voice, so familiar and yet strange, and by my own words, which have materialized from nowhere.

And then he is charging, hacking at me wildly, and I am forced back along the hedgerow: until I lose my footing over a protruding root and topple headlong into the mud and bramble—

whereupon my opponent falls on what's left of my sword and is promptly run through, his entrails unspooling like loops of linked sausage and his eyes turning to empty glass.

At length he says, "We kill ourselves," and laughs, even as I push him off me.

And then we just lay there, staring at the sky, neither of us saying anything, as our blood pools together and spirals down the slope. As the clouds continue to rumble—pouring rain into our dying eyes.

The diver trembles violently as I shake the vision off.

… repeat, *Zebra One* to Diver 7, are you all right?

I feel my leg through my flight suit, half expecting it to be flayed wide open—but I am unharmed, of course.

Roger that, *Zebra One*. However I am experiencing turbulence I cannot account for—what can you tell me?

There is a long pause which is pregnant with static, after which *Zebra One* responds, choppily, Diver 7 ... *Zebra One*. Be advised ... some kind of anomaly. We are working ... before it effects the mirrors. Please ...

And then they are gone.

I am gone, too. At least, I am no longer in the cockpit. Instead, I awaken from a dream I cannot remember in a place I have never been—no, I can see now that is incorrect. I am *home,* still sequestered in the dingy sleeping quarters at the very back of the Temple—where I have remained now for three days without benefit of food or water, and where I shall stay—unto death, if necessary—until Rue Umbra shows me His face.

Until He Who Created Everything bestows upon me the gift of His Holy visage.

"Master Hezekiah ... the Artifact is ready."

"Bring it to me, Jocasta. I will view it here in my chambers."

"Yes, Master."

I rise and swing my legs out of bed, and am startled briefly by my reflection in the bureau mirror. For it seems at first that I am someone—*something*—else; someone/something alien, with a gray, rumpled body and a face that is smooth like glass. Then it is gone and I see only myself: the green scales, the angled brow, the tired eyes of the High Priest of Samara.

At length Jocasta re-enters the room and places the box on the rug at my feet. "It is my hope—*our* hope, Master, the entire congregation's—that you will end your fast soon. May Rue Umbra light your way."

He moves to leave but hesitates, pausing in the doorway. "It is also hoped ... that you will be careful. This so-called Artifact—it is not of this world."

Then he is gone and I am alone with the box, the box containing the meteor which has somehow survived its entry into our atmosphere. The hollow meteor with the strange runes printed on its surface (at least, that is how it has been described to me). The thing whose existence is responsible for my crisis of faith.

Show me, Oh Highest One. Send me a sign. Reveal to me, your faithful servant, the naked face of God.

But Rue Umbra is silent as I open the box and lift out the Artifact, and proceed to examine it by the dim light of the candles. Nor is the object so unfathomable as I'd presumed: for it is clearly something designed to protect the head, similar in many respects to our Centurions' helmets (although charred and blackened from its journey through the atmosphere) and composed of materials I have never seen; some of which glow at the touch of my fingers and cause the Artifact to hum and to vibrate ...

Show me your face, Oh Lord, so that I may believe again!

But in the end there is nothing, only silence, as a glassy shield lowers smoothly and locks into place. As I stare into its curved, indigo-blue surface—which has become a kind of looking glass, a mirror—and see only myself, Hezekiah. Only the High Priest of Samara laid low by his fast.

Something is wrong. This much is clear as I stir from the vision and find the diver shaking— shaking as though it might fly apart any moment. *Zebra One,* meanwhile, is talking at me through my headset:

... get it back. We're trying ... but ... long shot. Repeat: we have ... return mirror. It's just ...

Again, damn you! You're breaking up. What about the mirror?

… has failed. We are trying—

But they are gone—and I am alone. Alone against the ergosphere, whose end must surely be near. Alone—in light of the mirror's failure—against the event horizon, beyond which lies Hell itself.

I pause, feeling it again. As though someone were in the cave with me, as though someone were watching.

I look to the mouth of the cavern, beyond which the snow continues to fall. No, it is nothing—the wind, perhaps, coursing through the opening.

I return to my work, continuing the stroke which will complete our leader (his snout blue with war paint, his shoulders broad and hairy), knowing he will be pleased. For I have captured him in truth—as well as the spirit of his hunt—captured him so that he might live for all time. And yet, as the winds moan and the torches falter, the feeling I am not alone persists, so that I again look to the door of the cave, and this time—someone is there.

The hominid doesn't move, doesn't seem to breathe, as I look at him, and for an instant I think, *Dr. Livingstone, I presume.* Then I laugh a little behind my visor, marveling that I can do so under the circumstances, and take a step forward, eliciting a growl from the creature I would not want to hear twice.

I hold, looking back at the diver—which is suspended nose-down in the middle of the air—before turning again to regard the creature and his art … only to find them gone, replaced by a very old man in what appears to be a Tudor-style study parlor.

"Livingstone, Einstein, Hezekiah, we've been them all, at one time or another." He begins moving toward me, casually. "You are ... Diver 7. I presume."

I just look at him, saying nothing. Behind him is a blackboard which runs floor to ceiling and wall to wall, and is crowded with equations. Noticing my gaze, he says, "Ah, yes. Well. The hominid has his work, and I have mine."

He stops within a few feet of me, examining my flight suit. "Your helmet. You won't be needing it."

I look at him for what seems a long time. At last I reach up and trigger the visor, which glides up and out of the way, and take a deep breath. The air is fine.

"Where am I?" I ask, glancing about the room, noting its exotic décor: a red, cactus-like plant (without needles) which looks as though it belongs at the bottom of an alien sea; a black and silver obelisk the height of a man; a polished suit of armor standing sentinel in a corner. "And who are you?"

The old man smiles, warmly, compassionately. "I should have thought you'd have guessed. As for where, why, you're stone cold dead in the middle of a blue hole. Where else? The mirrors, alas, have failed—but you knew that already. No, what you really want to know is … what does it all mean? The Hole, the visions, everything. Isn't that right, Diver 7?"

I look at the old man expectantly.

"Beats the hell out of me," he says, and moves toward the blackboard. "A blue hole is where mathematics go to die. No. What I have left is only conjecture, speculation—metaphysics rather than physics, notes as opposed to a complete script." He puts his hands on his hips, examining his formulas, and exhales, warily. "Of the trail of ink there is no end."

At length he begins moving again, pacing beyond the red plant and the black and silver obelisk, past the suit of armor which gleams like gold in the umber firelight. "Say, just say, for the sake of argument, that the Buddhists are right, and that reincarnation is real. And that its purpose is to evolve souls, to grow them—from the first spark of sentience to something approaching divinity. Would you allow that this was a worthy end to our travails?"

I don't say anything, only continue to watch him.

"Say, too, that these incarnations are infinite, or nearly so, occurring not just in this universe but a *multiverse,* so that, in time, we have experienced creation from every window and every door, every viewpoint—in short, we have been everyone and everything. *Mmm?* Shall we say it?"

He stops and turns around, begins pacing back toward me. "And that, as we reach the point of infinite progression, we begin to, slide, if you will, back and forth amongst our lifetimes—

putting the lesson together, as it were, making of it a sphere, rather than a line, compressing everything into an infinitely dense mass, an Alpha and Omega, a singularity such as is found in the heart of our blue hole. Would you say then that we had solved the riddle of its phantasmagorias?"

He pauses not three feet away and I just look at him: the tired eyes, the deep wrinkles and crow's feet—at last, I understand.

I lift off my helmet.

"I was you, once," I say. "We were … We will …"

He nods, slowly. "Not only us but all men, all sentient beings. Nothing is wasted."

My mind reels. "But … The Hole. My diver. It took those things to—"

He laughs suddenly. "Oh, that. Why, that's just a happy coincidence. You still don't understand, do you? You never needed the ship, or the vortex. You—we—were ready. Our infinite progression had reached—"

"Madness," I say. "Shadows within shadows."

But he is gone, replaced by Hezekiah. "It's the shadows that exist," he says, and I understand him perfectly in spite of his alien tongue. "The objects that create them; those are the illusions. Put another way: The ghost is real—the machine is not. Now—it is time."

And I am back in the cave, standing so close to the hominid I can smell him, watching him rub chalk on the stone, watching him create entire worlds. Until he looks at me sidelong and hands me the tool—thoughtfully, knowingly—as if he were encouraging me. As if he were saying: *You too can do it. You, too, are the Creator.*

Until I close my fingers on the chalk and everything fades to black.

And that blackness becomes Light.

I am become the White Fountain, the creator of worlds—the Big Bang which will expand outward, creating a new universe. Nor has the previous universe ceased to exist; for it dreams behind us on the other side of the Hole—its galaxies and star systems safely intact, its sentience growing by leaps and bounds.

Meanwhile, even amidst the crash and swirl of creation, I have remained—the godhead of an entirely new paradigm; the observer, and yet, somehow, the observed; the ghost in the rapidly expanding machine. Nor has every vestige of my former self been annihilated; for something has survived the explosion which even now hurtles outward into the maelstrom, spinning, tumbling, drifting ever further. For a billion years, it drifts, until, caught by a mid-size world's gravitational pull, it falls like a shooting star into an alien sea—a sea as red as blood—whereupon, again, it *drifts*.

Until it is retrieved from the water by a pair of eager hands—four-fingered hands—which grip the helmet firmly and place it into the boat, after which it is passed from one being to the other like the physical manifestation of a riddle, and finally put into a box.

Where it will remain—its secrets safe, its numeral '07' unseen—until delivered to the priest.

COUNTRY ROADS

"What'd you think?" I asked the bouncer—a gargantuan brother named Pinky; I didn't ask—on the way out, even as the jukebox began to play and the room began to return to normal, meaning loud.

"Hmph," he hmphed, staring straight ahead, keeping an eye on the boys in the MAGA hats. "I think you're lucky to be getting out of here alive."

"That's live comedy," I said—a little dickishly, now that I remember it. "It's no country for snowflakes. This brother brings it."

Call it a manic response to the thrill of the kill—because that's precisely what I'd done, killed it—though not so manic that I didn't ask him for an escort to my car.

He lingered, seeming pensive, as I got in and started the engine—enough so that I rolled down my window and asked him, "You really didn't like it, did you?"

He shrugged his massive shoulders. "My job is to spot trouble and eliminate it. Not to stir it up. But I do think … you said you were from New York?"

"I live there, that's right. Going home to visit family. Thought I'd line up some gigs along the way."

The man laughed a little. "That's right. You mentioned that in your routine. 'Haven't left my borough since those Mexicans flew them planes into the towers'—that was good."

I looked at him expectantly, wanting to know what it was he thought.

"Oh. It's just that … Well, you should get out of New York more. See the country. Be good for your comedy."

I wasn't sure how to take that. "Yeah. Well. Keep an eye on those rednecks. At least until I'm down the road?"

He nodded as I put the car in gear. "There won't be any more trouble. That I can guarantee."

I gave him the Peace sign.

And then I was off—into the Kentucky night which sweated and lay silent across the fields. Into a damp fog which reminded me of New York—and was at the same time completely foreign.

It didn't take long to start comparing the bucolic beauty of the state by day, with its rolling horse farms and verdant, bluegrass pastures, with its indistinctiveness at night. It was like driving anywhere, even upstate New York (except for the complete lack of other vehicles and the plethora of Donald Trump campaign signs, which seemed to stand sentinel in every other field). To tell the truth, I was beginning to nod off when a headlight appeared in my rear-view mirror—just one, a motorcycle, maybe, or a car with a burned-out lamp—and began closing the distance between us. It's funny because I remember thinking distinctly that it was moving too fast—a cop, maybe—which bore out quickly as the little sun grew—resolving itself, at length, into the working headlamp of a dirty 4x4 pickup. A pickup now tailgating me at sixty-five miles-per-hour.

You got anything else to say, Lib-tard? Maybe you've got something to say about my girlfriend. Don't be shy. I'm sure we all want to hear it.

I thought that was your wingman.

Keep talking ...

There was a pronounced jolt as the bumper of the truck hit my car, hard enough that it skewed a little on the damp pavement, and my heart leapt into my throat. Jesus, was it possible? It had been two hours since that exchange, two hours and a junction, there was no way—

Again the bumpers collided, and again there was a jolt.

Tell her you're sorry.

The truck veered into the oncoming lane suddenly, accelerating, and I was forced to do likewise—I didn't want them beside me. Didn't want to know if they had weapons or not. Didn't want—

Who? Your service animal? Or its mother?

I floored it as the truck's battered quarter panel appeared outside my open window, hoping the little Camry's V6 would open up, hoping it had more power than it seemed. It did—and I launched forward, causing the front of the truck to slide back, and the scenery to blur past with dizzying speed. I recall slapping the steering wheel like a pimply kid in his first car. *Eat my dust, suckers! I'll see you in Hell!*

But the old pickup only roared forward like a rocket, instantly drawing alongside. That was the moment, of course. The moment I realized just how much trouble I was in. For what I saw outside my window was not just some car full of idiots. Rather, it was like something from a horror movie—*Duel*, maybe, of fucking *Birth of a Nation*. What I saw outside my window was a truck full of hooded men—like KKK members, only wearing brown instead of white—like scarecrows having sprung to life from the fields. Or executioners.

There were six of them in total, more than had been present in the bar (not that it mattered, they would have rounded up others, I was sure). The important thing is that it *was* them—the MAGA crew—of that I had little doubt. Three of them were crowded into the cab while three others rode in the payload—all of them wearing crudely-stitched burlap hoods—and each brandishing some form of weapon, whether that meant a pistol or a rifle or a rusty pitchfork. The truck, meanwhile, was right out of central casting—I'd seen others like it in the red states I'd already passed through. You've seen them too: those jacked-up tanks with the huge tires and pig-ear smoke stacks (their way of saying "fuck you" to the environmentalists), and the twin flags crackling in their payloads—usually an American and a "Don't Tread on Me," but sometimes a bona fide Confederate Southern cross, which is what this one had, along with one I couldn't clearly see. All I can say for certain is that the men in the back put down their weapons as I watched and appeared to fiddle with something in the payload—I really couldn't say because I had to look away in order to focus on the road.

Meanwhile it didn't exactly surprise me to see that I—we—were going about 90 miles-per-hour—the fastest I'd ever traveled in a moving vehicle, and a speed at which the Camry had become dangerously unstable. I thought then of my decision when I was young to never own a firearm, and laughed a little at my own expense. Only then (and how I'd managed to not think of it until that instant remains a mystery) did it finally occur to me: my bloody phone was right there on the passenger seat!

The truck's engine roared and its flags crackled as I snatched the thing up and dialed 911, putting it on speaker so that I might better focus on the road, not to mention re-grip the wheel firmly in both hands.

A moment later it came: "911, what's the address of your emergency?"

I stammered and babbled before managing, "Old State Route 51—yes—Old State Route 51, between Danville and Tomlinson. I'm being pursued by a truck full of masked men, h-heavily armed. Let me repeat that; they are heavily arm—"

"What is the make and model of the truck?"

I glanced out the window. "I—I don't know. A Ford, maybe. Yes, a Ford, I'm certain of it. It's dark green and has flags flying from the back. One of them's a Confederate. I—"

I noticed movement and focused on the man nearest me—by the window in the truck's passenger seat—saw him training his pistol on, on …

My tire. My fucking front tire!

I let off the gas immediately and slowed down before veering into the lane behind them, even as the operator asked calmly, "Are you able to see the license number? If so, read it to me—as carefully as you can. Are they Kentucky plates?"

I was distracted by the men in the payload, who appeared to be lifting something heavy, but quickly focused on the plate. "Yes. Kentucky 527 CXS, Franklin County." I squinted in the fog. The lettering didn't look right. "I—I think it's been altered. I'm following as close as I dare, and it looks like—"

"You are behind them?"

"Yes. One of them was—"

"Sir, be advised that units are on the way and that you are not to pursue. Repeat, do not pursue. Pull over immediately and wait for officers to arrive. What is the make and model of your vehicle?"

"I—it's a blue Toyota—a Camry. 2004, I think. I'm—I'm slowing down. But so are they. There's men in the payload. It, it almost …"

I was about to say that it looked like they were lifting, well, a trough, to be frank, one of those big aluminum vats used to water horses, when the men heave-hoed the thing twice ... and sent its contents hurling toward my windshield. At which point the thick, viscous stuff hit the glass like a hammer—exploding everywhere—and turned the world black.

Black and blood red.

I must have waited there on the shoulder of the road for an hour, at least, during which time I fetched a road flare from the trunk—the closest thing I had to a weapon, sadly—as well as the 5-gallon plastic gas can (which was full, like the Camry's tank, because the car's fuel gauge didn't work), although as to why I grabbed it I can't really say. Maybe I just wanted it close so I could refuel quickly if it became necessary. Maybe I already had some divination of an outcome—whether I was consciously aware of it or not.

What I *was* certain of is that no cops had shown up, nor whirred past through the fog with their lights flashing chaotically, in the entire time I'd been waiting. Likewise, my phone had remained silent—as if my call for help had simply fallen through the cracks, or never happened at all. One thing, for sure, *had* happened: a trough full of blood—animal blood, presumably—had been hurled at my windshield, and it had made one hell of a mess, a mess the worn wipers had been inadequate to clear, thus I'd had to clean the glass manually with wiper fluid and a towel.

I waited another five minutes before tentatively buckling my seatbelt and starting the car, peering down the road intensely, seeking any sign of the truck. It looked clear. Even the fog had lifted somewhat.

At last I edged onto the road, picking up speed gradually, using my blinker, which gave me a little laugh, increasing to 55 miles-per-hour. A portion of my act came unbidden to my mind—I was looking for what could have motivated them to murder, I suppose, beyond merely insulting someone's girlfriend—the Cavalcade of Clichés, I called it. It was the portion of the act where I'd recite, in rapid-fire succession, every bad joke anyone had ever told on a subject: in this case, Southerners. Rednecks.

What's the difference between Virginia and West Virginia? In Virginia, Moosehead is a beer. In West Virginia it's a misdemeanor.

How can you tell if a redneck is married? There are tobacco spit stains on both sides of his truck.

What can a pizza do that a redneck can't? Feed a family of four.

It was all pretty innocuous stuff, hardly anything to go to war over. And yet there had been a moment—just before my confrontation with the heckler—a moment that had struck me as strange, even by Bible Belt standards. It had occurred just after I'd segued into a semi-serious bit on Civil War monuments and social justice—a bit in which I'd gone so far as to defend the Antifa protestors who'd toppled the Silent Sam statue at Chapel Hill.

I remembered it clearly because the room had fallen absolutely silent—so silent I heard the big bouncer—Pinky, God bless him—say, and I mean softly, "Move on."

Don't get me wrong. I was used to this sort of response when I challenged audience expectations. Indeed, had I been anywhere else—a college town, say—I would have been pontificating on the evils of political correctness—if for no other reason that when it comes to making an audience more malleable, a little cognitive dissonance can go a long way. But this felt as though I'd committed a real breach, had somehow touched on something I didn't and couldn't understand—and, moreover, had done so perhaps from a position of pure malice. Either way, the trouble had started almost immediately after, and, although I'd rebounded by show's end—some might even say spectacularly—with a flurry of region-specific crowd pleasers, I never got the sense that I'd been forgiven for what I'd said.

I listened in near silence as the radials droned against the surface of the road.

Or, Bright Boy—they were just a bunch of racist pieces of shit. I mean, surely that was possible, in the *fucking South*? Yes—even in 2019?

Forget it, I told myself, as the fog continued to lift and it became clear the truck was gone. It's over.

Whatever it had been.

It would be difficult to describe just how close they'd come to killing us all—how little time I'd had to yank the wheel and hit the brakes in those first awful seconds after they'd shot from the sideroad. All I know for certain is that I ended up facing in the opposite direction—even while they careened into the trees on the other side of the road … where they quickly reversed, massive tires spinning, and narrowly missed me yet again—for I'd stepped on the gas and chirped out of their way.

And then we were right back where we'd started (only traveling in the opposite direction), piling down Old State Route 51 with our vehicles side by side and the truck's chrome stacks belching black smoke into the night. And I saw in the vespertine darkness what I couldn't have seen before—which was the flag previously blocked to me snapping and crackling in the wind. And I saw, too, that it was identical and yet radically different, for its colors were black, red, and green, and this filled me with a terror I could not define—in part because the combined colors felt alien and yet familiar, and in part because its very existence made of me an illiterate. Made me question if I knew anything beyond my borough in New York at all.

Not that I had time to dwell on it, for when next I glanced at the truck and its occupants I saw that the man in the passenger seat and the men in the payload had, all of them, pointed their firearms at me.

What I did next surprised even myself, for I sideswiped them without even thinking about it, and such was the impact that one of the men toppled from the payload and fell face-first into my window—where the whites of his eyes shown wide through the eyeholes of his hood—before he fell against the rushing pavement with a sickening slap-crunch and was instantly gone behind us. And then they were veering into *me*—although by intention or loss of control I couldn't possibly say—and I very nearly careened from the road—and yet, somehow, did not.

That was the moment, I think. The moment I knew what I was going to do. It was also the moment that the man in the truck's passenger seat shot clean through the door into my leg, spattering the upholstery with blood, and making me feel as if I might black out any second.

It's funny, because the gas can was in my hand and its lid taken off before I'd even consciously decided to grab it, nor did I hesitate before hurling it into the truck's cab and reaching for the road flare—which I quickly managed to uncap while driving and swipe against its striker. Then the Camry's interior filled with orange-white light and I threw the thing—threw it with everything I had, and before I even knew if I'd gotten it into the truck the Ford's cab exploded into something like the sun.

And then we were both skittering out of control, the burning truck toward the left shoulder and I toward the right, and the last thing I thought of before everything went black was how little things had changed in the fifty-two years I'd walked the planet. How little things had changed since Jesse Washington and Mary Turner and Emmett Till and James Chaney. Since Martin Luther King. Since 1981 and Michael Donald.

"Wake up, Yankee."

A voice in the blackness. A rich voice, a radio voice. A voice I had heard before.

"I'm not going to tell you again, New York. Wake up. I got something to tell you."

I opened my eyes, slowly, realizing my entire body had gone numb. The speaker's face swam into focus.

"I guess you're not feeling so smart now—are you?"

It would be hard to say what I noticed first, the fact that half his face was gone and that his brain was partially exposed, or that he was training a pistol on me, or that I knew him—had known him since before starting my act. All I know is that I recognized him immediately and that he was perfectly correct: I *didn't* feel very smart ... didn't feel much of anything now that the Camry and I were sort of one big casserole and the big bouncer was glaring at me from just outside my window.

"You—you *really* didn't like it, did you?" I gurgled—and laughed suddenly, causing a fit of convulsive coughing.

"Smart to the end, I guess," he said, and coughed a little himself, bringing up blood. I looked to where his head had been nearly cleaved in two. "What's gray and black and red all over?"

"Shut up and listen."

"Your brain," I said.

He jammed the muzzle of the gun against my forehead. "What's it feel like? Knowing you're going to where there ain't no God and there ain't no New York, just you and your Yankee friends, burning for what you did?"

I must have just looked at him.

"Knowing you pissed your life away telling jokes—while never once having stood for anything … never once having sacrificed. What'd y'all think, that no negro served? That no negro ever died in that slaughter you called a war or bonded with his white brothers while defending his homeland?" He *hmphed,* something I found incredibly funny considering half his head was gone. "Maybe they didn't fight, but they were there—scouting, cooking, running supply—there when the battle against federal tyranny was joined, and there when it was lost. And they are here, now, in the bodies of their descendants—working as cops and dispatchers and magistrates; working as bouncers in roadside bars. And they will tolerate no more of the desecration of their … Of their …"

And then he was gone, just like that, the pistol tumbling and clattering against the ground, his body slumping unceremoniously out of sight. And it struck me that the 911 operator I had spoken to had almost certainly been one of them—not one of them in the truck, of course, but one of them in spirit—the unlikely sons of the confederacy. Or *something.*

And it struck me too that I would never know: no more than I would know why some people were convinced that Barack Obama or the U.N. or fucking Michael Moore were coming for their guns or that a global conspiracy of patriarchs ruled the world or that we were all being routinely poisoned by chem trails—people built mythologies, it was what they did, and more, was I any different? Hadn't I been equally convinced that a group of drunken Trump fans had decided to chase me down and kill me because they'd taken umbrage with my act?

You should get out of New York more. See the country. Be good for your comedy.

I laughed a little at that, tasting my own blood.

Get out of New York. Get out of our boroughs.

Oh vey.

Shouldn't we all.

Made in United States
Orlando, FL
30 May 2024